MW01173180

PUBLIC DOMAIN: Introduction to Huna by Max Freedom Long

Edited By Dave S. Romain

Cover Design: Dave S. Romain

ISBN 13: 978-1-9992983-2-6

ISBN 10: 1-9992983-2-2

Issued: November 2020

CHAPTER-ONE

THE INVESTIGATION OF HUNA
AND HOW IT CAME ABOUT

During the past century investigations have been made of native magic in Africa, India and other parts of the world. Spiritualistic phenomena have been, certified as genuine and studied painstakingly by over a hundred recognized scientists. Religions have been surveyed and the instant or nearly instant miraculous healing at Lourdes verified. But from all these studies and efforts there has come nothing faintly resembling a definite basic system, philosophy, theory, or psycho-religious science which would explain, even in the most general terms, the phenomena of the various fields. In fact, investigations in these fields began to arrive at a stalemate several years ago. New discoveries have been conspicuously lacking. Meanwhile, in the years following 1880, in the little noticed field of Polynesia, there was begun an investigation which, after seventy years, has at last produced a general theory that promises to break the stalemate and provide answers for a host of puzzling questions. This investigation was begun by Dr. William Tufts Brigham, long curator of the Bishop Museum in Honolulu. In Hawaii there were, up to about 1900, many kahunas, or native priests, who, although outlawed, worked among their fellow Hawaiians as healers of body and purse, or used the dread "death prayers". Some fire-walked over lava overflows which were cooled barely enough to bear their weight. A few demonstrated instant healing, and the young scientist was fortunate enough to be able to observe and study a case in which a lad, dead from drowning for sixteen hours, was brought back to life through a use of native magic. After fire-walking himself under the protection of the kahunas, and verifying the healing and other phenomena which they produced, Dr. Brigham came to the conclusion that behind these and similar activities there must be a single basic scientific system, like a string upon which the beads of religion, psychic phenomena, psychology and native magic were strung. He redoubled his efforts to discover this system. The kahunas, (the word means "keeper of the Secret") had a strict cult of secrecy. They would tell him very little about their lore. What little they did tell was so unfamiliar and so muddled, because of the use of unintelligible Hawaiian words, that he could make almost nothing of it. The "Anaana" form of the "death prayer", however, was studied and partly explained in terms of spiritism. In the year 1919 I went to Dr. Brigham to ask what scientific information might be available concerning the activities of the kahunas, of whom I had heard many wild tales during my three years in the Islands. A friendship developed, and I was invited to make use of all the materials which he had assembled, and to continue the study if I could. I was trained in the matter of correct scientific approach to this unfamiliar field and its materials. I had many cases of kahuna healing and other activities described in great detail for my benefit, and discussed these cases with my mentor in the light of what was known in the psycho-sciences at that time — which was very nearly as much as is known in these stalemated days. Upon one set of conclusions, Dr. Brigham was insistent:

1. That there must be some form, or monad or entity of consciousness which was in man or without him, and which the kahunas were able to contact through ceremonial or prayer.

2. This unidentified consciousness could use an unidentified force in such a way as to control temperature in fire-walking or make changes in physical matter in instant healing. As these conclusions pointed inevitably to a basic system of a psycho-religious nature, it was necessary to decide that there was much still remaining to be discovered in the new science of Psychology, and much to be explained in the phenomena of Psychic Science. In the absence of even the slightest clue to what these things might be, I would certainly have refused to

take part in such a hopeless investigation had it not been for one outstanding fact. This was the fact that this secret and mysterious basic system was not a matter of empty words and theorizing. **IT WORKED**. It was alive and kicking, even if in its death struggle. Dr. Brigham had been suspiciously careful in verifying the materials of the investigation. I had already verified some lesser things (and was soon to verify some most important accomplishments of the kahunas). The thing could not be ignored. There was something right there under our very noses which **WORKED**, and even though it evaded our grasp, it seemed inconceivable that, with modern science so far advanced, we should not ultimately get to the bottom of the mystery. A few years later, Dr. Brigham died at a ripe old age, much honored, but still with a burning curiosity unsatisfied. I continued the work, collecting more materials in the field, watching for any new development in the psycho-sciences which might give me a clue to the "Secret" of the kahunas, and going absurdly far afield at times hoping to find a glimmer of light on the baffling problems. Finally, by 1935, new clues had been discovered which led directly to the basic system. In due time it was possible to explain in fairly general terms a part of the basic theory and its methods of application. It was the ancient "Secret" of Huna, of the kahunas. The new clues came largely through a study of the meanings of the roots of the Hawaiian words. By the summer of 1935 sufficient progress had been made toward understanding the ancient lore that a report seemed in order. I wrote this report and it was published in 1936, in London, by Rider, under the title of **RECOVERING THE ANCIENT MAGIC**. The study and its materials were described and tentative conclusions given. Assistance was asked from any reader of the report who might have knowledge of this or related fields or of similar materials. One reader was W. R.

Stewart, retired newspaper correspondent, living in England. He had been engaged in his youth in an effort to learn native magic from an isolated Berber tribe in the Atlas Mountains in North Africa. There he had studied beliefs and practices which, years later, upon reading the report, he saw stemmed from the same original source. The words used in naming the elements in the Berber version of the system had been said to belong to a secret priestly language, but, upon comparison to similar Hawaiian words, proved to be identical except for slight changes which may be ascribed to the differences in dialect. Such language differences are found among the eleven Polynesian tribal branches in the Pacific. The common language of the Berber tribe was a degraded Turki. Stewart joined the investigation, which by that time, 1937, had reached an advanced stage. He added his findings and contributed in many other ways. Unfortunately, his death in 1943 robbed the work of his aid, but, when World War II ended, the basic system was deemed to have been developed as far as would be possible until it could be put to the acid test of practical use. Efforts to apply the basic system and duplicate the most valued parts of kahuna practice are expected to correct errors and to make possible the further perfecting of the system. To this end experimental groups are forming (late in 1945) in Los Angeles, with other groups to be formed in Australia and England. While this outline report of the investigation is intended as a partial text for the use of experimental groups, it will also be made available to the public. A much fuller and more detailed account of the long investigation is planned when the last stage — the experimental stage — has added its quota.

CHAPTER - TWO

FROM FIRE WALKING TO INSTANT HEALING

Fire-walking (including all fire-immunity) and instant healing make very good starting points for an explanation of the ancient Polynesian or pre-Egyptian lore called "The Secret", or, in Hawaiian, Huna. There is nothing at all mysterious in bare feet or in glowing coals, hot stones or hot lava flows. There is nothing mysterious in a broken bone or a cancer. Our materials are open to examination. The feet may be examined after contact with the fire in fire-walks. The broken bone or the cancerous tissue which has been instantly healed remains simple bone and tissue. Let us first consider a few cases of fire-walking, keeping in mind two questions:

(1) What god is prayed to for fire-immunity, and

(2) What form of "purification from sin", if any, is necessary before one can fire-walk?

FIRE-WALKING CASES FOR CONSIDERATION

Kuda Bux fire-walked in 1936 before the University of London Council for Psychical Research. He was a native of India, of the Mohammedan faith. Before his demonstration he closed his eyes, raised a hand, and recited a prayer from the Koran. In Burma, where a gentleman took motion pictures of mass fire-walking in which some natives were badly burned but many were unscathed, years of fasting and other purifying practices were the preparation for the feat.

PUBLISHER'S NOTE

On Friday, March 7, 1975 Vernon Craig of Booster, Ohio established a world record for fire walking at the Phoenix Psychic Seminar, Phoenix, Arizona. Official temperatures sampled at three locations averaged 1,220 degrees Fahrenheit in a 20-foot pit of glowing wood coals. Better known as KOMAR, Craig holds numerous world records for his feats.

In the Philippines the Igorot's have for centuries done admirable fire-walking. A group of them came to Seattle and performed almost daily at a fair. These people used to be famous for head hunting as well as fire-walking. In Polynesia, fire-walking is done after offering a ritual prayer to a "native god". Dr. Hill, of the University of Southern California reports seeing a young white man try to fire-walk on the same hot stones after the natives were finished. He prayed to his God, concentrated his thoughts, and started across. A dog fight broke out beside the pit and distracted his attention for a moment. In that moment he jerked up a foot, which later showed a large blister, but continued the fire-walk successfully to the end. A white man who is a professional entertainer eats live coals, drinks down boiling water, grips red-hot iron bars in his teeth and bends the ends up and down, also lets the iron-cutting flame of a welding torch play repeatedly on the inside of his mouth and throat. He says he is conscious of an invisible entity or spirit presiding over fire, and that he makes request for protection which is instantly granted. At Palm Springs a few years ago a desert Indian lad took large coals from a fire and held them in his hands, holding them out to tourists in the audience and challenging them to take the coals offered them. Little is known of the preparations made by the fire-handlers of Indian tribes, but they also have their prayers, rites and gods. In Hawaii, up to the year 1900, fire-walking was done on overflows of molten lava as soon as they were cooled sufficiently to hold the weight of large stones thrown on them. Dr. Brigham fire-walked successfully over such a lava bed under the protection of three native priests or kahunas. He refused to remove his heavy boots and during the passage over the lava these were burned from his feet, as were his two pairs of heavy socks. These natives prayed to some god, but Dr. Brigham could not learn about its nature. Outwardly it was the 'goddess of the volcanoes, Pele, about whom native legends continue to collect even today. If instant healing had been known only in Hawaii, no matter how carefully it had been studied and verified there by Dr. Brigham and others, there might be some excuse for those who make a flat denial of such a possibility. But, since another and far better-known scientist, Dr. Alexis Carrel, has added his verification in his book, MAN,

THE UNKNOWN, there is no longer justification for any denial of the basic fact that instant healing is possible. It was brought about in Hawaii by the kahunas and is still being brought about by mysterious agencies at sacred shrines in various parts of the world. As all roads once led to Rome, so all indications point to the existence of one basic system behind this phenomenon, and to the undeniable fact that it is a workable system. Instant healing cannot be repeated over and over on the same broken bone or cancer, therefore the patient has no chance to become practiced in his part, as does the fire-walker for whom the gods perform a similar magic, over and over, upon request. Instant healing, while similar in its mechanisms, is rare. It is best studied in cases in which a definite part of the body is healed. Casual ills may be suspected of just happening to disappear of their own accord.

CASES OF INSTANT HEALING FOR CONSIDERATION

The best instances of instant or miraculous healing have been verified and studied at the shrine at Lourdes, France. Typical cases are those of the healing of spinal deformities or cancerous tissues. The healing may be instant or may take up to three days. Prayer has usually been addressed to God or Christ or the patron saint of the shrine. The person healed may not be praying for his or her own healing at the time, but someone in the vicinity is thought to be always at prayer at the instant of healing. Various preparations by way of "purification from sin" are made by the patients as a rule. In Hawaii the kahunas healed instantly in some cases. Dr. Brigham observed two cases of instant healing. Broken bones were roughly set and a muttered prayer made. The patient was then declared healed and immediately could use the injured limb. J. A. K. Combs of Honolulu, observed the use of similar methods when his wife's kahuna grandmother healed a compound fracture of the ankle in this way. The patient was a native man, very kindly and well liked, but very drunk at the time of the injury and during the healing, which was accomplished within a few minutes of the accident. (He had stepped from a standing automobile into a ditch filled with very soft sand.) In the Hawaiian cases there was sometimes instant healing accomplished with no preparation of the patient, although in cases of long-standing illness rites of purification were almost always used as a preliminary. We may sum up by saying that no particular "god" has to be prayed to. No particular religious beliefs are needed. The ideas of what makes a "sin" may vary, as may the degrees of effort to gain purification. In some instances, purification is not necessary. Also, mortal values are a matter of geography as seen in the case of the head hunting fire-walkers. While we are not ready just yet to go into the matter of "purification from sin", it may be noted that the only "sin" recognized by Huna is that of hurting another unjustly. The kindly Hawaiian had imbibed too freely at the beach party but had hurt no one and was not found in need of purification. The healings accredited to Jesus are not at all incredible in the light of Huna. Sometimes he forgave the sins of the ones about to be healed and sometimes he did not.

THE THREE THINGS NECESSARY TO INSTANT HEALING
Three things are involved in the mechanism of instant healing and fire-walking as described in Huna.

1. Some intelligence wise enough to bring about the healing or temperature changes when requested to do so.

2. Some force or power to be used in making the changes.

3. The substances which are changed in the healing process. Also, the substances which are involved in the making and offering of the prayer.

SECTION I. THE ELEMENT OF CONSCIOUSNESS
The three are the basic triad: Mind-Force-Matter. There are nine elements in man, in the Huna system, with the human physical body to make a tenth.

MIND IS DIVIDED INTO A TRIAD OF THREE GRADES OF CONSCIOUSNESS. FORCE IS DIVIDED INTO A TRIAD OF THREE VOLTAGES OF FORCE. MATTER IS DIVIDED INTO A TRIAD OF THREE DENSITIES OF A CERTAIN KIND OF THIN MATTER.

The concept is simple and well ordered. We cannot use an effort of will or even hypnotic suggestion to the subconscious to cause fire-immunity or instant healing, so we must look for a Higher Consciousness which is wiser and more powerful than we are. Immediately we think of God. But this answer needs more understanding of the nature of God than most of us possess. Let us examine the god-concept of the reconstructed HUNA. We begin with the idea that our minds are unable to grasp the true nature of God. The ancient kahunas said He was a triune being and that between Him and man were several grades of Conscious Beings. The grade of beings just a step above man were so difficult to imagine and understand that efforts to understand still higher levels were given up as hopeless. It was thought that, if mankind needed to have contact with the still higher levels, the closer gods would see to it that the higher gods were properly approached. That simplifies matters greatly. Now we can consider what has been learned about the beings in the level just above ours. By this we mean beings able to use a form of thinking or mentation next in line of superiority to ours.

SEEING INTO THE FUTURE is something we can try to do hours on end and fail to do. Our hypnotized subjects cannot do it upon order. But often the future is glimpsed by hypnotized subjects, by normal waking persons or in our dreams. Seeing into the future is not our ability; it is an ability of the god just above us. It has some mysterious way of seeing into the future, and it gives us our premonitions, dreams and visions at unpredictable times, never directly to the conscious mind, but by way of the subconscious. (These two parts of mind are not permanently united but are separate entities, as we shall see in due time.)

MAKING THE FUTURE is another activity assigned to the Conscious Beings just above our level. The ancients called these Beings the Aumakuas. In psychology we may call them the Superconscious. A good term is Higher Self. Considered as a combined community of spirits or entities, they can be our Christ Consciousness or Universal Mind. (Man is a trinity composed of three "selves" or spirits, the subconscious self, the conscious self and the superconscious self.)

The **FUTURE** is seen in Huna to be constructed by the Higher Self. It lays out the main points in the life of the individual of which it is a part. But the day-to-day future is built by taking the thoughts, hopes, fears and plans of the lower two selves, the subconscious and conscious, and using them as figurative "seeds" from which to grow the events of our tomorrows. We have FREE WILL in so far as we are allowed to think what we will, get into trouble, and do quite as we please in furnishing the materials which go (as if automatically) to make our future conditions and life events. This answers the problem of free will and predestination. Except for the determination of the long-term events of our lives, such as birth and race and place, we exercise free will.

INSTANT HEALING is obtained by deciding that we want a future in which we are not ill but healed. If we ask the High Self to heal a broken bone instantly, and it is done, we can say that the High Self changed the future instantly for us in so far as having a broken bone is concerned. We may say the same of fire-walking. There are other things involved in such matters, of course, but the point to be made here is that we, as **FREE AGENTS**, must decide what we want, and hold that decision, as the initial step in getting help from the High Self.

(This applies to the **HEALING OF PURSE AND CIRCUMSTANCES ALSO**— a branch of healing even more important than bodily healing.)

THE FORM OF MENTATION used by the High Self includes ability to see that part of the future **WHICH HAS BEEN CRYSTALLIZED OR BUILT** for nation or man. There is much of the future of the individual created from day to day and changed from day to day as we change our plans and thoughts, so the **UNCRYSTALLIZED** or un-built part of the future cannot be seen. The past can be seen. Things at a distance can be seen. The High Self seems not to be hampered by what we call "reason" or "memory", which are the forms of mentation used by the low and middle selves (subconscious and conscious). We, as middle or conscious-mind selves, cannot understand a form of mentation higher than our own. We can only observe the things the High Self is able to do with its superior form of thinking ability, then draw what conclusions we may. God is unknowable to us. The High Self can be known in part. It is much like the relation between a man and his dog. The man looks after the dog and plans the "musts" in the dog's life and activities. But the dog can do as he pleases for the most part. He may get into trouble, and then, if he is smart, run to his master for help. The master understands his dog. The dog knows a lot about his master, but because he has only a dog mind, many of the activities and purposes of the master must remain mysteries. This dog-master relation is also a good illustration of the relation of the subconscious self to the conscious self.

SECTION 2. THE ELEMENT OF FORCE
We have seen that the High Self is the element of consciousness involved in instant healing and fire-immunity. Let us now consider the force it uses.

IN HUNA ALL THINGS ARE TRIUNE.
There is always:
(1) a conscious being using

(2) a force or power, to work with

(3) some form of matter, be it dense or etheric.

VITAL FORCE IS THE FORCE USED BY THE HIGH SELF. The triune man has three voltages of this electro-vital force. In the laboratory we have measured vital force in the body. It is of the three to four-million-volt level. Similar force is found in the brain, but its voltage has been stepped up a million volts to the next higher level. The High Self does not live in the body with the low and middle selves and so has not had its voltage of vital force recognized as yet by laboratory men. Huna recognizes three levels, grades, or voltages of vital force, a voltage for each of the three selves or entities. The voltage used by the High Self is higher than that used as "hypnotic will" by the middle self, so must fall in the five to six million or "atom smashing" range.

ATOM SMASHING voltages of electro-vital force, used by the High Self, are considered to be the answer to how heat is controlled in fire-walking, or both heat and cold are regulated when the material substances in a bone break are **DISSOLVED TO ETHERIC FORM AND THEN RE-SOLIDIFIED** as an unbroken bone.

APPORTS in spiritualistic seances are produced by thinning out the substance of the object or living thing, then transporting it to some other place and resolidifying the materials. Spirits of the dead are able to get the aid of their High Self to produce apports and the phenomena of "transportation, levitation, materialization", etc. The spirits of the dead are no more able to sense and recognize and understand the High Self than we, the living, are. They have tried to explain the phenomena which they are instrumental in producing, but their guesses do not agree. (In learning to use the Huna system it is to be expected that we, the living, will work with the Higher Self and produce such phenomena without the necessity of depending on the dead.) The VITAL FORCE is made in quantity on the earth level. Plants have it. Animals and men generate it from the foods they use. The low self in the body generates and uses the LOW **VOLTAGE OF VITAL FORCE**. This level of force is taken by the middle self and its voltage stepped up to the **MIDDLE VOLTAGE OF VITAL FORCE** which is used as the "will" to control the low self. The High Self draws vital force from the body and steps its voltages up to the **HIGH VOLTAGE OF VITAL FORCE** to use in instant healing and other things.

SECTION 3. THE ELEMENT OF MATTER

We have seen the grade of consciousness and the voltage of vital force involved in fire-immunity and instant healing. Now we come to the third element of the triad, **MATTER.**

There are two grades of matter or substance to be considered. First there is the substance in a broken bone or a diseased or deformed portion of the body. This is the easily understood matter which is dissolved into invisible etheric form and re-solidified as normal or "healed" bodily portions. The second grade of matter is that thin etheric substance of which bodies are made for ghosts. Everything has a thin, shadowy body which is a **MOLD OF EVERY MICROSCOPIC PART OF IT.**

Each of the three selves has a shadowy body. Consciousness and vital force cannot work without material, so even the High Self has to have a body, even if it be but an etheric one. During life the low and middle selves interpenetrate the gross physical body with their shadowy bodies. At death the shadowy bodies are withdrawn and lived in on "the other side". The High Self lives in its shadowy body all the time, never entering the physical body, but often touching it, especially during sleep. The halo above the heads of the saints in old paintings represented the High Self hovering over the saint in its shadowy body.

THE SUBSTANCE OF WHICH THE SHADOWY BODIES ARE MADE is ideal for the storage of supplies of vital force. It also is a perfect conductor. The spirits of the dead can take vital force from the living and store it in their shadowy bodies. With it they produce psychic phenomena of limited kinds, e.g. moving tables.

The **SHADOWY BODY OF THE LOW SELF** is a mold of every tissue of the physical body. This mold can be withdrawn almost completely from the body for a time without the materials of the tissues beginning to disintegrate. THIS MOLD is not tightly filled. It has no fixed form but can be stretched, elongated or made a different size.

IT IS UNBREAKABLE. A bone may break but not the shadowy body part that is the mold of that broken part. Cancerous tissues may invade the shadowy mold but not change it.

SO, THE PROCESS OF INSTANT HEALING IS ONE IN WHICH THE MOLD IS EMPTIED OF BROKEN OR DISEASED TISSUES AND IS REFILLED WITH BASIC SUBSTANCES TO CONFORM TO THE UNINJURED MOLD.

It may be added that the High Self can do many other things. It can, either directly or through its associates of its high level, exercise control over weather conditions or over animal, insect or plant life. We cannot understand just how this control is exerted, but we can observe results obtained, which is, for practical purposes, fairly satisfactory. The kahuna of the Berber tribe known to W. R. Stewart, stated that, according to tribal history, the Great Pyramid in Egypt had been built by her kahuna ancestors. They got Higher Selves and associates of that level to cut the stone and transport it into place in the pyramid structure. Stone of a similar perfect cutting and placing is to be seen in Mexico and places farther south. While we have no way to verify statements such as those of the Berber kahuna, we know from the finding of modern Psychic

Science that similar performances on a smaller scale are possible. Parts of stones have been used as apports; the parts being cut off with no seeming difficulty. The cut is not a break but leaves a smooth and sometimes almost polished surface.

CHAPTER - THREE
HOW THE AID OF THE HIGH SELF IS OBTAINED

In the psycho-sciences, all of which are new and incomplete, we find no recognition of the High Self, or its voltage of vital force. Naturally, there has been no effort made to find a way of making contact with the High Self or of getting its aid. In Religion, however, there are remains of a mechanism of prayer. It is to prayer that we must look when we turn back to Huna for a working explanation. This is the very heart of the basic system and it is with the prayer mechanism that experimental groups are to learn to work. The High Self does not reside in the physical body, but outside of it. We do not know just where. But when we pray to it for aid, we must be able to make contact with it and get our prayer considered. For this reason, our first question is one of how the two lower selves can communicate with the High Self. All communication between sentient beings must be done through thoughts, or words representing thoughts, or through thought symbols such as writing. Telepathy is a direct transfer of thoughts, and is the method used in prayer to the High Self. Everything has its shadowy body, including thoughts. Thinking is done with the use of vital force, and vital force works only through matter, dense or eth-eric. Each thought, as it is formulated either by the low or middle self, or the two working in cooperation, is impressed on a microscopic portion of the substance of the low self's shadowy body. **THIS IS THEN A THOUGHT FORM.**

Our thoughts come in trains or clusters and make bunches of thought forms like clusters of grapes. Each cluster is tied to the next by a tiny invisible thread of the same etheric substance. When we finish thinking a thought and it passes from the focus of the conscious mind self, it is taken by the subconscious mind self and stored as a memory. The storage place of these memory thought forms is not the physical tissues of the brain, but the shadowy body of the low or subconscious self. When we die the low self leaves the body in its shadowy body and is able to take along our memories because they are stored in the shadowy body and so do not decay with the brain tissues. When a telepathic message of thought forms is transmitted, the sender does not give up his thought form or "forget" it. He may be said to keep a carbon copy for his memory files. In mind reading the mind reader reaches out and examines the thoughts or memories of another and brings back duplicates of them, otherwise the person whose mind was read would cease to have as a memory the item "read". The reason telepathy and mind reading are rare is that both must be done by the low self. The middle self can direct the low self to send or receive a message but cannot do it for itself. In hypnosis the operator reaches out silently or makes contact through the use of words, in either case planting thought forms in the low self of the subject. These may or may not be accepted and acted upon. As Dr. Rhine has pointed out in his work with telepathy, there can be no broadcast of thoughts in purely electric form because the matter of distance makes no appreciable difference, as it certainly would if electric power were sent out as from a station. (We will see soon the Huna explanation of this matter.)

COMMUNICATION WITH THE HIGH SELF occurs naturally during sleep. We know that in sleep we frequently get dreams of the future. Remembering that the High Self alone can see into the future, we conclude that in sleep there is a telepathic communication with the High Self. Or there may be intimate contact between the High Self in its shadowy body and our own low self in its shadowy body, in which case our stored thought forms could be inspected on the spot. It is in this contact at night that most of the thoughts of our days are averaged by the High Self and used in some mysterious mechanism to materialize corresponding events and conditions in our future. If we fear something, that fear may become a part of our future. If we change our plans and desires frequently, our futures become a jumble of conditions. Psychologists have come to believe that perhaps as high as ninety per cent of our ills and accidents can be traced back to thoughts from which they must have originated. If we build a picture of our future with bright plans and high faith, we must take care not to kick over the fragile "seed" structure by allowing ourselves a day of discouragement in which we doubt the efficacy of the practice of "holding the thought". Our entire lives are predicted by our thoughts. We may say that every thought is a prayer because it eventually is used by the High Self to determine the nature of the future being almost automatically built. This is a hard idea to connect with the belief in a loving god or High Self. We would expect love to cause the bad to be cast aside and only the good used in making a pleasant future. Experience teaches us that we are served with both good and bad. As free agents we think into form the seeds of our futures. Only when we correct our thinking or ask the High Self to wipe out the bad and materialize a new and good set of thought forms can we get assistance. If it were necessary only to "hold" good thoughts to get them eventually accepted by the High Self and materialized into facts in our future, we would have a rather simple mechanism to use.

But there are obstacles, **THE OBSTACLES TO COMMUNICATION** are the complexed ideas or fixations of guilt or unworthiness, sin, doubt, fear and so on. The low self stubbornly holds to all its habits of thought. A habit of thought is partly the result of having very large clusters of strong old thought forms lodged in the memory. The instant we begin an action, mental or physical, which calls up those habit memories, we find a fixed set of ideas which are difficult to break down and replace. For example, those of us who have been reared in Christian beliefs frequently have complexes built in childhood with ideas of "sin" and guilt. We may have had an emotional strain at a time when we decided not to "sell all and give to the poor".

Remember that when we make the thought forms of a "prayer" and try to communicate with the High Self to deliver the "prayer" directly, we **MUST CALL ON THE LOW SELF TO TOUCH THE HIGH SELF AND DELIVER**

THE PRAYER. IF THE LOW SELF HAS A COMPLEX OF SIN-GUILT OR UNWORTHINESS, OR DOUBT, IT WILL NOT DELIVER THE PRAYER. Or, it may deliver the prayer but ruin it by the inclusion of thought forms of doubt, fear and endless other contaminating things. We have the task of clearing out of the low entity any fixations. The kahunas called this process, "Clearing the Path". This was the "path" of the prayer from the low self to the High.

THE FIRST STEP IN PREPARATION FOR COMMUNICATION with the High Self is to get the path of communication cleared. Several things must be kept in mind at this point. First, we must realize that man cannot "sin" against God or the High Self. We are not big enough or able enough. Neither can the flowers or insects or animals' sin against Higher Beings.

The **ONLY SIN** recognized in Huna is that of **HURTING ANOTHER.** And this sin cannot be wiped off (as long as it continues to hurt) by any means other than expiation. We must change our idea of the morals of the High Self as we go along. Our morals are filled with dogmas which must be examined and put aside if not valid. The "Do unto others. . ." is sufficient. It is the kahuna, Christian and Buddhist command. The idea of Karma in which we pay in one incarnation for the sins of another, is not valid. It must be greatly changed (as must the general idea of reincarnation) to match the reconstructed Huna.

IF WE HAVE HURT SOMEONE unjustly, there is nothing we can do to convince our logical middle self that we are not guilty, except to go and make amends for the hurt. Then WE know we are in the clear, but in the low self, there may often remain weak or strong resultant guilt or unworthiness fixations. These must be drained off or sublimated to open the path.

THE HUNA METHOD OF DRAINING OFF A COMPLEX of this nature is one which was probably connected with the basic idea of sacrifice in the early days. The low self is illogical. It can only remember and use animal-like reason. It is stubborn. It can best be rid of guilt complex thought forms by the use of physical acts or stimuli accompanied by suggestion or auto suggestion of a mild nature. The kahunas usually made certain that all hurts to others had been expiated before going on to the complexes. To get rid of these the patient was made to observe a fast or do deeds of service for others or give alms until it hurt. These things were sacrifices. They were done with the thought of making redress for sins of omission or commission. The Roman Catholic Church uses penances in the same way. The Christian rites of the confessional, penance and baptism for the remission or cleansing away of sin are all duplications of ancient kahuna practices. If the priests could use light suggestions while sprinkling the individual with holy water, the water would act as a physical stimulus and help impress the low self that it was being cleansed of its sins. Other physical stimuli were used with their mild suggestion by the Kahunas. Anything will do if it is physically impressive and contains a picture of something such as cleansing, washing or freeing.

THE USE OF A PHYSICAL STIMULUS, or a series of penances which act as a series of stimuli, is a very great help in getting suggestion to take effect on the low self. The use of suggestion by our psychologists would be greatly improved in healing if such stimuli were invented to fit various cases, and always used. Just to pray for forgiveness is not usually enough.

A TEST FOR A CLEAR PATH is the test of prayer. The low self is always linked up with the consciousness of the middle self and feeding up memories to help furnish ideas and words with which to pray.

If, therefore, when we pray, there is a guilt complex in the low self; our

"CONSCIENCE" WILL USUALLY TROUBLE US. We will be like a naughty child called before a parent, who will hang his head in guilt and remain sullen and silent, but, if the child has been a "good boy", especially if he has just finished an arduous task to please the parent, there is a joyous approach with an expectancy of praise and reward-well-earned. It is the same with the man who has fasted and otherwise cleansed his low self of guilts. The path is open to the Heavenly Father-Mother, the High Self (and through that to God if need be). If we have a correctly made prayer-thought-form with no doubts and fears ruining it, we have then the open path of communication to the High Self and can go forward in full faith and confidence. If, however, we have not learned to reach out and touch the High Self successfully, to give it our prayer, all we can do is to "pray constantly" never varying our prayer, and hope that when the High Self takes our daily thoughts to use to construct our future, our prayer will be included without having been too much altered by the low self.

The Huna **TELEGRAPH WIRE USED IN TELEPATHY AND IN COMMUNICATION WITH THE HIGH SELF** is next on the list of things which must be understood and used if instant answers to prayer are to be obtained. The shadowy body of the low self is not only a mold of all the tissues of the body, storage place of memories, a conductor of vital force; but it is the means of connecting us with things and people. It is sticky and when we see anything, it extends out with the sight and sticks a tiny thread of the invisible substance to the things seen. We shake hands and a thread connects us with the person whose hand we have touched. We touch anything and, in this way, establish a connection with it. Such connecting threads of shadowy body substance last for a great length of time and tie us into our surroundings so to speak. The sound of Dunninger's voice over the radio is followed back by the recipient in the audience to make a thread of contact with the mind of the broadcaster. Telepathic communication over fourteen thousand miles of distance between Sir Hubert Wilkins and his New York friend, Harold Sherman, was possible because they had between them threads of this kind.

These **THREADS OF SHADOWY BODY SUBSTANCE** act as guides when we order our low selves to reach out and touch someone. Contact once made, the thread is momentarily strengthened by pouring into it more shadowy body substance. This is projected from the shadowy body of the low self and the kahunas speak of it figuratively as "sticking out a finger". Once the thread is thus reinforced, it is a perfect conductor for vital force, and on

A **CURRENT OR FLOW OF VITAL FORCE CAN BE CARRIED THOUGHT FORMS.** A portion of the sensory organisms can be removed from the physical organs and projected to the thing touched, through the projecting "finger". (The sensory organs are duplicated in the shadowy body of the low self. After death we have the use of all the senses.) Things at a distance can be seen, touched, tasted, heard and smelled. These threads bind the clusters of thought forms together as we store them in series in our memories. "Association" of memories is a matter of being able to pull the strings attached to one memory and draw up all associated memories.

A **THREAD OR CORD OF THREADS** connects us with objects and people often touched. Mediums sometimes can feel these coming from the region of the solar plexus. The mechanism of psychometry is to touch an object, then cause the low self to stick out a "finger" and follow the threads which are attached to the object, back to the owner. The owner may be around the world in distance, or dead and living in his shadowy body on "the other side", but he can be touched and his thoughts and memories inspected, his appearance rioted and his surroundings sensed or seen.

THREADS OF SHADOWY BODY SUBSTANCE CONNECT US WITH THE HIGH SELF, and, if the low self has no hindering guilt fixations, it can be trained to put out a "finger" and contact the High Self, then send a flow of vital force along the enlarged thread to carry the thought forms of the prepared prayer.

THE REACTION OF THE HIGH SELF seems to be automatic. Perhaps there is more discretion used than we suspect in answering these prayers, but in fire-handling the High Self very seldom fails the performer who depends on instant and constant answers to mental prayers for protection. The prayers themselves become unconscious in so far as the low self has become trained to touch the High Self and present the often-used set of thought forms of the prayer for protection. This is a prayer rapport, so to speak. When the hem of Jesus' robe was touched, the healing was possibly accomplished by this habitual prayer action of the low self. It is recorded that Jesus felt the "virtue" go out from him and knew that someone had been healed.

THIS "VIRTUE" would be vital force, according to Huna. The High Self seems to need little vital force for use on its own level, but when it changes physical, or dense materials, it needs a good force supply. This is usually taken from the individual making the prayer. The kahunas used to order the low self to generate an extra amount of the vital force and send it flowing to the High Self with the prayer. There is nearly always a sensation of electric tingle as the vital force is drawn or sent out, usually as soon as contact is established. In fact, the tingle is the common indicator of contact with the High Self. The vital force has, of course, to be stepped up in voltage by the High Self to be used. (Vital force of any voltage, when used through the shadowy bodies or their protrusions, seems almost intelligent in its actions, although we know that the intelligence must be resident in the being directing the activity.)

Here are the several steps to be taken in making the Huna "prayer" for instant healing, fire-immunity, change in the future, etc.

(1) The low self must be trained to put out a "finger" or protrusion of its shadowy body and follow the invisible threads which will guide it to the High Self.

(2) It must be trained to send thought forms along the paths of contact, as in telepathy and mind reading.

(3) It should be trained to generate an extra supply of vital force on command, then to send it along the paths of contact as needed.

(4) If contact with the High Self is not made, the path must be cleared by removing guilt complexes from the low self.

(5) The prayer must be most carefully made, after due consideration of possible unexpected consequences should the prayer be answered. When final decisions are reached as to what is desired, the prayer is to be formed by wording it aloud three times over. Using the will to impress the prayer on the low self and to build strong thought form clusters.

(6) The prayer when thus made is held in mind and the low self is ordered to reach out and touch the High Self. When an answering electric tingle is felt, the prayer is recalled or even spoken again aloud so that it can be sent to the High Self with the extra supply of vital force needed to materialize the thought forms of the prayer into immediate or future events.

IF A PRAYER IS MADE FOR THE HEALING OF ANOTHER, this individual must be cleansed of all guilt complexes as a preliminary act, otherwise his low self will prevent the healing.

CHAPTER - FOUR

EXPERIMENTATION AND ITS
PROBLEMS. MORE DETAILS OF THE
HUNA SYSTEM.

In actual practice it is anticipated that some individuals will excel in the work of calling down the actual healing action from the High Self. Others may be unable to do this, but will be able to get patients ready for the actual healing. All experimenters will usually try to learn the simple movements of mind first, but will at the same time remember the necessity of working toward the end of contact with the High Self. Experimenters with mediumistic ability will sometimes be needed to work with the less psychic members. It is probable that in cases of obsession, or attack by angry spirits from "the other side", the psychic members will enlist the help of their spirit guides to "see" the spirit causing the trouble, and to watch progressive results when exorcism is attempted by other healers. This is a special branch of the work and will be in the hands of those especially qualified to undertake it. Obsession and the various degrees of "split personality" are accounted for by the Huna system (as it stands at this writing) in fair detail, but the study must be continued in this branch with experimentation helping to feel the way. It is clear that the low and middle selves are often separated from each other at death, and that, singly, they may attach themselves as "split personalities" to the living, or may completely obsess an individual. If there is amnesia in which a new and different set of memories arrive, it can be assumed that the low self has been displaced. Only this self can remember and store memories in its shadowy body. If there is a change in "personality" but not in memories, only a middle self has been displaced. If both personality and memory are seen to change, there is a full exchange of selves in the body. Frequently the middle self is forced to leave the body because of disease or injury, while the low self remains, caring for the body and remembering, but with no middle self there is no inductive or higher reason, so the insane patient is "irrational".

In cases where there is this irrational type of insanity, and/or a complete loss of earlier memories, it would appear to be a definite matter of the human low and middle selves abandoning a body (or being ousted from it in some way) and the body falling into the possession of something which may:

(1) be subhuman, or

(2) may be a very young or injured, human low self.

Mediums (and even the insane themselves, when recovering or when their obsession begins) describe seeing these obsessing spirits. Some are distorted or grotesque or dwarfed, some blind, some with features hardly human. The Huna system presents a theory of evolution in which units of consciousness evolve upward step by step from the group units of rocks and waters, through the vegetable kingdom, to insects, birds and animals. Man has his three selves or separate spirits, and each learns the lessons of its level and then graduates into the next level above. As an illustration we may call the low self a first-grade student, the middle self a second grader, and the High Self a third grader. Each self is associated with the self, next above it in the triune man. In this way the middle self trains the low self so that it eventually is ready to become the middle self of a savage, and, when graduation time comes, is born into a savage body. It is then a middle self and is ready to begin learning, through several lives, the use of inductive reason. In this new savage body, there is a new low self which has just graduated from the animal kingdom. It may have been the self in a very intelligent pet dog, and it begins its schooling under the new middle self. With and above them is a High Self who, according to Huna, has not just graduated into that level, but who has been taking a long training in being the over soul of the lower kingdoms, perhaps as a group soul. (This group soul idea is not greatly important to practical work, but is very interesting.) The High Self is called "the trustworthy parental   self", and is supposed to have to demonstrate its trustworthiness before undertaking the supervision of human low and middle selves. From this school of selves there are those who "play hooky". By accident or otherwise the low and middle selves sometimes get separated at the time of death, or when insanity is caused by disease or injury and the middle self is forced out of the body. The low selves, when alone and not supervised by a middle self, on "the other side" are given to efforts to get back into a body as parts of "split personalities", or as obsessing spirits. They attend seances and pretend to be normal two-self ghosts. They can read the minds and memories of sitters and will pretend to be a dead friend or relative, even some famous historical character. They are unable to use inductive reason and, while usually as friendly as a stray dog trying to find a new master, eagerly say what they think the sitter would like to hear. Frequently they are very hard to recognize for what they are, and the bright banner of Spiritualism has been besmirched by their lack of logic, lies, and trickery. A most surprising situation is sometimes found in instances where the low self of some advanced individual has, after or before the time of physical death, in some way learned to contact the High Self and present to it both a thought form prayer and a flow of vital force. (Here we see another evidence of the High Self's almost automatic response to this stimulus.) This low self has the memories of its past life and so does not forget the mechanism it has learned to use. It is, however, irrational and childish. It first finds a living person from which it can steal vital force, usually an adolescent boy or girl, and then gets into mischief. It makes its prayers and becomes more than the ordinary poltergeist (who merely uses stolen vital force to break or throw things). It becomes the super-poltergeist who can get fire-immunity, or who can apport fire or water or stones, or do other things. In Italy in recent years a child and her grandmother were bothered by such a spirit. Fire was constantly being kindled near them or in their beds or clothing. In other cases, water was apported and used to drench the victims of the joke at odd times. In France paving bricks were apported and hurled in a stream at a certain house for some days and nights. They were apported through the roof and fell thudding inside the rooms, but they were dematerialized as swiftly, so the piles of stones never grew high. Similar cases of stone throwing have been reported from the wilds of Malaya and Java. It is evident, however, that the High Self exercises some control over such performances, because no permanent injury is done those upon whom the tricks are played. (If a low self is using stolen vital force without contact with its High Self, it may move objects and sometimes come very near to injuring the living.) The High Self allows us far more use of free will than the average parent allows a child. In the animal world free will is allowed on a grand scale and animal eats animal, but the evolution of the units of consciousness is not greatly delayed. There are always fresh bodies to enter. Instincts, however, rule the lower kingdoms and in obeying the instincts little free will is allowed. Birds build nests after certain set patterns and in season fly north or south. There is order behind the seeming confusion caused by the evolution upwards toward the stage when a complete free will can be obtained. This final achievement may come after graduation from the High Self level — our minds are unable to reach that far and so we cannot be sure. We are going to make the effort to learn to use Huna, and regain the direct help of the High Self and its associates of its high level. It is very important that we come to know as much as possible of the actions of the High Self in the production of psychic phenomena, especially physical phenomena. Spirits who attend seances are not always what we should expect them to have become before they could contact, and gain the help of, the High Self. The spirit, known as John King, was given to boasting that he had been a murderous pirate in life. He was a rowdy who was not even slightly sanctimonious. His morals might well have been suspect. But, like the low self super-poltergeists just discussed, he was able to get High Self help upon request and produce exciting phenomena. Nearly all the phenomena of Psychic Science (excepting premonitions, ghostly appearances and the like) have been produced by spirits who are able to contact a living medium and use her vital force or that of a circle. A very few of these spirits are able to produce physical phenomena, (apports, materialization, etc.) but those must have learned in some haphazard way to touch the High Self and present the right thought forms, with vital force sufficient to get phenomena produced. The point is that none of these spirits knows Huna. They have all tried more or less to answer the questions of the living as to how they produce the phenomena. Their answers have been as impractical (and often as illogical) as those given by living psychical researchers. In a hundred years of speculation not a single theory has been put forward which would furnish an acceptable explanation of more than a few simple items in psychic phenomena. In offering a general theory that covers the field except for the mechanisms of a few still-dark corners, Huna promises to break the stalemate that has stopped Psychic Science for three decades. The same can be said of our badly stalemated Psychology and its allied sciences. Religion has been stalemated for some time, the older forms for many centuries, and the newer forms which included modern psychological discoveries (New Thought, Christian Science, Unity, etc.) for about as long as Psychology and Psychic Science have been bogged down. In the new religious forms the mechanisms and theories of Huna were partly, if indistinctly, grasped with the result that instances of healing body or circumstances are frequently recorded. Here we find much evidence of the fact that Huna in white hands (the darker races are naturally more psychic, which is an advantage in some practices) will work. If so much has been done with such incomplete knowledge, a vastly greater accomplishment should be made possible now that we have more complete understanding of elements and mechanisms. We should soon be producing the desirable phenomena of the seance room without calling on the spirits of the dead for help and without the need for a medium. We will endeavor to use the circle as a source of vital force, each sitter donating a little, and the leader of the group creating the thought forms of the "prayer", making touch with the High Self and getting its assistance (and that of its fellows) in healing projects. In England, during World War II, an experimental group endeavored to use Huna methods through the ritual of the Church to open the doors of heaven and invite the Higher Selves to take a hand in ordering affairs in the world. Unfortunately, it is impossible to know whether fortuitous turns in the struggle were aided or caused by such efforts. It was a splendid gamble and, considering the world situation since the war, might well be undertaken on a large scale lest the free will allowed us on this level bring us to ultimate social or even physical disaster. We do not know to what extent we can depend upon the Universal Associate High Selves (or Beings above that) to help us work out a social system which will provide justice, freedom, and an order in which we help one another instead of competing selfishly and with the fierceness of the animal kingdom. The English group tried to call for the prophesied "World Judgment" to balance race injustices, no matter which races were found at fault and caused to pay a price for bettered world conditions. We can be safe in saying that, for a beginning effort, the experimental groups —when organized to work on a large scale — cannot go wrong in formulating a "prayer" envisioning reforms which would tally with the Golden Rule. Even the negative version, "Do not unto others. . ." would be a great tool if we could use it. Later, as this study of Huna progresses, every effort must be made to see whether or not we can get from the High Selves glimpse of a perfect plan for a world social organization, or, failing that, help in formulating a plan of our own which we can perfect in the course of time. The Huna lore of old pointed to normal living as the great criterion. Each living thing was thought to be in its intended stage of evolution, and there was sufficient time for all to grow upward. Family life was good. All normal living was good. There was no doctrine of asceticism and self-denial. There was plenty of time to grow to the stage where graduation into the next level of consciousness was due. This is in strong contrast with certain dogmas which crept into Christianity and other early religions. The contrast needs to be stressed. All of us cannot "sell all and give to the poor", else we would have nothing but poor beggars. All of us cannot leave friends and families and take the yellow robe and beggars' bowl of Buddhism.

All of us cannot become hermits living half-starved in caves hoping to find God. The practice, so common in India, of leaving friends and family at forty and retiring to monastic life in order to "see God", is not justified in Huna. In Huna, one teaches or helps or heals, each according to his ability, even when he has come to be able to touch the High Self, whether once in a long time, or at will.

CHAPTER - FIVE

HUNA AND THE SEVERAL RELIGIONS

The ancient system of Huna seems to have been known in full form in Egypt at the time of the building of the Great Pyramid. This would give us an approximate date of 2600 B. C. (There may have been an "Atlantean" origin of Huna as far back as 50,000 B. C. This is all purely speculative.) After the building of the Great Pyramid, named "The Light", according to the legendary oral history of the Berber kahunas, the Secret Lore, or "Light" as it was also called, disappeared with the tribes who knew it and who migrated largely to the Pacific, or, in the case of one tribe, to the Atlas Mountain region of North Africa. In Egypt the Huna lore was kept secret and the language (later the Polynesian) was never reduced to any form of writing. This language bears every evidence of having been the one used when terms for the several elements in Huna were invented. Small common root words were united to make longer words, each root describing some feature of the thing named. (Or some long and complicated meanings were represented by short symbol words used as a part of longer terms.) It is, therefore, evident that peoples speaking what is now a Polynesian language were the original holders of the knowledge of Huna. Otherwise the words would be artificial, or substitutes, and their root structure not uniformly a source of the full word's meaning. The tribes who lived in or around Egypt migrated, touching India and other lands and leaving behind them parts of the original Huna which can still be identified in various religions. In India there is a great similarity between the idea of pranic energy and the three voltages of vital force used by the three human selves. Perhaps the division of the pranas into forty-odd kinds (for taste, sight, hearing, etc.) came later when the practical use of Huna was forgotten (if ever fully known). The same may be said about the ideas relating to the three shadowy bodies inhabited by the three selves of man. In modern Theosophy, which is drawn from the several religious systems of India, we find the three shadowy bodies expanded to seven, of which some are supposed to house elements related to emotions, or mind, or to be of an "astral shell" type. The idea of thought forms was well preserved, and, while not known in such detail as in Huna, was recognizable in terms of the Old Secret. The Bhagavad Gita treats of our High Self, and of the two lower selves considered as a single self. The triune idea was perhaps known after a fashion, but was applied more to the gods. The doctrines of reincarnation and karma, while enlarged, as were the ideas of prana and the shadowy bodies, retained some of the original significance. In Huna the matter of evolution through a series of incarnations was part of the general system, but the theory was made to fit the changes brought about in the course of graduation from one level of consciousness to the next. It is apparent that it is not the same man who incarnates after a graduation in which the middle and High Self have stepped up, leaving the low self to take over as the middle self in the next incarnation, and a new low self to join the man from the animal level. The involutionary idea of a man being forced back to become an animal in some incarnation because of "sin" has no part in Huna, so far as has been ascertained. The doctrine of karma applies, in Huna, only to the law of cause and effect as it operates under the free will in single incarnation. After death the man makes a thought-form world or "purgatory" in which he lives as in a dream, and there such things as he may have on his conscience haunt him until he has made what amounts to a retribution. As memories are not carried from incarnation to incarnation, and as no mechanism has been discovered for carrying the results of past sins or good deeds across, it would seem that what karma there may be must be in the hands of the High Self. Perhaps the High Self sees that we are punished for hurts done others in past incarnation, but in any event, the idea of karma would have to be made to apply individually to the three selves of man, as in the idea of reincarnation. It is evident that the law of justice in the animal world (to which the physical body and low self seem to belong) is quite different from the law of justice conforming to the inductive reasoning powers of the middle self. The justice of the level of the High Self is probably still different. Be that as it may, Huna recognizes no karmic law which says that a man must be forced to suffer from illness, accident or social tangles to expiate past-life karma. In Theosophy much stress has been placed on the Masters. Under Huna a master would be one who was able to contact the High Self and get help of a "miraculous" nature. It is unfortunate that so little can be learned about these highly evolved legendary men or their activities. It is, however, very possible that men can evolve, come to know the High Self, and graduate to the levels above in orderly fashion, and still have no definite and detailed knowledge of Huna. In all races we have had our saints who have reached their elevated state through a deeper inner realization of the great verities, rather than through what might be called a scientific understanding of themselves and their elements. In Christianity there is to be found much of the Huna lore, some things badly overlaid with dogma, or distorted, others in a surprisingly good state of preservation. With the beginnings of the early Churches, many rites and practices were adopted which, while not well described in the New Testament as it has come down to us, belonged to Huna. With the passage of time the rituals of the Church (Roman, Greek and derivative Churches), came to be used with little understanding of their original purpose. The injunction of Our Lord to go forth to all the world, healing and helping, could not be fully obeyed. The healing mechanisms were gradually lost until only their outward forms remained. After the Dark Ages there were many who sensed this lack in the Church, and who tried to get back to the early and more practical doctrines by fresh studies of the Bible. The protests against priests and rituals rose in volume and Protestant Churches were formed. In these the priests were discarded and the members tried to find God for themselves, through Jesus as the Son of God. The trend was back to the austerities. But still there was little healing of a predictable kind. In modern times the science of Psychology began to take wavering form soon after the discovery of mesmerism. Quimby, a New Englander, and after him, Mrs. Eddy, recognized and tried to use for healing the "Wisdom" and the "Power", which was a recognition of the High Self and its high voltage of vital force. Elements from Indian sources may have given the idea of "holding the thoughts", and a denial of unwanted conditions was used with even better results than might have been expected. In New Thought much the same methods were used, but with less drawing on Christianity in constructing new doctrines and dogmas. In many lesser Mental Science groups where a religious approach was kept, similar steps largely made possible by the advance of knowledge in the science of Psychology, and as this science became stalemated some decades back and could offer no more guidance, the modern religions also bogged down, and then began slowly to freeze their dogmas and reject outside ideas. For Christians, the understanding of Huna is not difficult. The teachings of Jesus have much in common with the older lore. Jesus demonstrated ability to contact the Father at will and, in explaining the miracles, pointed out the fact that it was through the Father that those things were possible. The kahunas believed that instant healing was possible only through the High Self, which was to them the Aumakua or "Older, most trustworthy, parental" Self. As the Christ, Jesus is often considered universal in nature. The kahunas believed that all High Selves were so closely related that they could react as one unit aggregate of consciousness, and thus take on the universal aspect, even while remaining individuals. Jesus was closely identified with the Father, being a very part of Him, or Son. The Father worked through him and seemed to be in him. This feeling that the High Self is inside one is explained in Huna as a sensation experienced when contact with the High Self is made, through the mechanism of the connecting thread or cord of shadowy body material. Thought forms of future events are brought to us from the High Self along this cord and are presented to the focus of consciousness, of the middle self, "inside" us. We do not get the impression that our premonitions or premonitory dreams come from without, but from within our own physical bodies in some mysterious way. (It may be, however, that, at rare intervals, the High Self actually may enter the physical body in its shadowy body.) Jesus told of the love and the joy of the Lord. Worshipers of many faiths have felt the sudden emotional surge of love, joy and devotion that comes to bless the devotee. The kahunas knew it. It is the reaction of the low self when able to contact the High Self. We, who are the middle selves, have no ability to cause emotion. That is part of the mentation peculiar to the low self. But we can and do share the emotions generated or felt by the low self. The joyous emotional up-surge, like the feeling of an electric tingle, are common indications that we are in contact with the High Self. This is our most tangible sensory proof of the verity of the High Self (or the "Comforter" of Christianity). The High Self is also the counterpart of the Holy Spirit in Christianity. In India a religious state known as samadhi is attained. It is this same emotional joy and love and devotion. But contact of this nature is not made through religion alone. The telepathic experimenters and others, working with psychic abilities, often report such contact. It is unpredictable in its coming, but unmistakable once it comes. In Upton Sinclair's book, "Mental Radio", his wife has been quoted as she writes of her methods of using telepathy. She speaks of the conscious mind and the subconscious, but knows another consciousness which she calls "The Deep Mind". She tells how she finds the telepathic impressions from the subconscious (our low self) dim, fragmentary, fleeting and not always accurate. But sometimes the "deep mind" seemed also to answer her questions, and its answers are unmistakable, clear and convincing. With these answers there comes a great feeling of "gladness ", and in describing this type of experience on page 201, she undoubtedly shows that she has frequently touched the High Self. In healing work, Jesus at times used a physical stimulus to accompany words and commands that unquestionably may have had strong powers of suggestion. Recall the blind eyes covered with a mud made of earth and spittle. This is similar to the kahuna use of a physical stimulus to accompany and strengthen suggestion. Jesus sometimes forgave the sins of those about to be healed, but not always (see the case of the blind man). The kahunas ordered their patients to make amends for hurts done others, then used some physical stimuli to aid suggestion in draining off guilt fixations — so that the low self of the patient would be restored to a condition in which it could be healed by the High Self. This condition was one in which the "path" of contact with the High Self was said to be "unblocked". It was the condition of feeling oneself cleansed of guilt. It was a condition necessary to the restoration of faith, without which no healing was thought possible. The concept of "salvation" is not a definite mechanism in Huna. It was believed that men could, however, be greatly helped and saved much stumbling about, if they could be told that there was a High Self and that it could be touched and asked for aid and for a certain degree of guidance-under-free-will. This belief was expanded in India to become the salvation to be obtained by breaking the chain of reincarnations. The grip of karma was to be broken through having all sins worn out by suffering. In Christianity we find only indefinite traces of the doctrine of reincarnation. Karma is found only in the day to day application of the law of atonement for sins. The Jews hoped for a Savior to redeem the race from bondage. The redemption in Christianity was from accumulated sin — a slightly similar idea to that of karma. Jesus, as the Christ, can well be understood in terms of Huna. In Huna we cannot pray directly to the Beings higher than the High Self. We must ask the High Self to exert its superior mind power in our behalf and, so to speak, send on any prayer or praise of ours which should go to God or Higher Beings. Christians are, likewise, directed to address all prayers to God through Christ. Jesus said that he would pray to the Father for the disciples, and in this aspect, he stood as the Christ or High Self, if we are to judge by the light of the Secret lore. The externals of the reconstructed Huna system are cold, but within lies all the possibilities of those deepest, warmest responses to the High Self. In the old religions, even when stripped of healing, there has remained something so mystical and deep that even when dimly sensed we are swept by waves of nostalgic longing to get back to some greater verity of being. The new psycho-religious system based on Huna and working through Huna Research Associates has been envisioned as one in which the lost things will again be known and used. In it we will perhaps get quickly back to those nearly lost verities of experience— restore our touch with the High Self, and through it with Ultimate God. To those of us for whom religion has been a deeply integrated part of our lives, the prospect of such a restoration has about it a breathless quality of expectation — a quality of upward surging. It will not need to be described for those who feel it for themselves.

CHAPTER SIX

THE EXPERIMENTAL APPROACH TO HUNA

The proof of the pudding is in the eating. The proof of the correctness of the reconstructed Huna system is its workability. Huna worked for the kahunas. It should work for us. A long and detailed explanation of how the conclusions concerning the elements of Huna were reached may be of academic interest in years to come; but at this time experimental groups have agreed to accept all conclusions as tentative and see if they are workable in practice. Additions and corrections to conclusions can best be made during and through experimentation. Very little has been learned about the methods used in former years to train the kahunas. In Hawaii the children were sometimes taken to the mountains by their kahuna teachers and taught the lore. But the only thing recorded was that the training began at about the age of thirteen, and that its first stage of success was indicated when the youngster could hold in his (or her) hand a small piece of fragile pumice stone, say a "prayer" and cause the stone to crumble into dusty particles without using physical force. In beginning her instruction of W. R. Stewart, the Berber kahuna gave daily talks on the legendary history of the tribe and began at the top of the theories by discussing the concepts of God, then of each level of consciousness and being below, bringing consciousness down to its deepest immersion in matter and starting it on the upward swing. At the beginning period of the training she took the young Englishman and her daughter to hilltops and there showed them how to contact the High Self level and the beings who directed lower forms of life. One day she asked that birds be instructed to gather at the hilltop, and very shortly a large number of birds of various kinds gathered. She asked the High Self to show itself as a form and they saw a dim outline of something that had a human face but a large bird-like body. Snakes were called together on another day, and within an hour a surprising number of them were to be observed on the rocks or soil or in the bushes. They did not come near the three who sat on the crest of the hill, and departed swiftly as at a given signal. No High Self was seen at that time. Stewart was unable to explain, in later years when telling of his experiences, why his teacher had not foreseen the danger of a stray bullet — the bullet which killed her before her instructions had reached the practical stage of training of her pupils. He expressed the opinion that she had failed to ask to be shown the future, not anticipating a danger so remote. An interesting point in the preliminary teaching of Huna theory was explained by this teacher. She said that it was taught that in the course of evolution the animal called man became ready, and then a god came down and assumed the place of a middle self, living inside the animal body, training the low self, and causing changes in the brain to enable inductive reason to be used, also the "will". The animal mate of the first human was soon put into a deep sleep and the High Self divided into male and female parts, the female part entering the female body. The teacher thought this old Huna legend was the original of the Adam and Eve story. She pointed out the significance of the division of the High Self, by saying that when it was divided into two parts to rule over two animals of opposite sexes, it lost its god-like powers. It could no longer see the future without help from above, nor could it change matter or directly control nature. This was, she thought, the original idea of a god incarnating in a man animal, and so making the supreme sacrifice of itself, to make possible the salvation or continuing upward evolution, of living things on the earth. When Stewart mentioned the idea of "soulmates" she said that all consciousness was male-female. Human bodies presided over by a mated pair of low selves came together only superficially. The middle selves could think identical thoughts and could come more closely together as High Selves a perfect union of consciousness. This interblending, she said, enabled the creative work of the highest order to take place. It was her practice to "pray" that her High Self Mother-Father parts come together to hear her further requests and take action of a "magical" nature on them. Continuing her* account of theory, she pointed out the fact that all telepathic and other actions of mind or shadowy body materials was greatly easier and more perfect on the level of the High Selves. It thus became possible for all High Selves to form a single interlocking unit (we would say a Christ Consciousness, or Universal Mind in our new Christian religions), but at the same time, paradoxically, the unit High Selves retained their individuality. Because of this close association of High Self units, the thoughts of people on the earth level were considered in their relations to others, and their combined thoughts evaluated to make their futures. The future of each person is dependent on what his associates, or even strangers, do as their individual futures are made for us in relation to our associates and through some form of cooperation of the High Selves of ourselves and associates. This rapidly becomes such an involved mechanism that we are forced to remember that we can have but a very vague understanding at best of the High Self and its powers and form of mentation. It is because of this inability to understand the High Self level and its ways of doing things that we make wild guesses, and these guesses become fresh dogmas which gradually snow under the basic things. In Hawaii from the time that Dr. Brigham began the present investigation, no kahuna ever revealed the Huna lore to any extent. They spoke of the two lower selves and of the High Self, which they referred to as one of the gods or "the god". Not GOD. W. R. Stewart made a study of the common and religious secret (Polynesian) language in order to understand his Berber teacher, and thus was told in detail the exact meaning of important words. But in Hawaii neither Dr. Brigham (nor later, the writer) could have understood the native words, even if used to explain Huna. (Of course, there were no counterpart words in English known to the kahunas which would have enabled them to describe the lore.) Missionaries, arriving in Hawaii in 1820, soon made a dictionary of Hawaiian words, but at that time there were no words in English for such things as the three selves and their shadowy bodies and the three voltages of vital force, nor for thought forms or invisible threads of shadowy substance. The words for the low, middle and High Self were, respectively, Unihipili, Uhane, and aumakua. In the dictionary (still in use today) these were assigned the meaning of some variety of ghost or spirit of one deceased. The three terms used for the three vital force voltages, low, middle and high, were, respectively, **Mana, Mana-Mana, and Mana Loa**. These were translated, in the order given:

(**1**) **"supernatural power"**

(**2**) **"to branch out and form several divisions" (which was the symbolic stepping up of voltage)**

(**3**) **"strongest or divine supernatural power". (Of interest here is the use of mana with the causative: hootnana, which means, "to worship".** This is another example of the kahuna use of words as symbols of more complicated mechanisms. This "worship" is the act of generating an extra supply of low voltage vital force, then making contact with the High Self, and presenting the prayer thought forms, with the supply of vital force, to be stepped up in voltage and used to materialize the prayer into fact.) It was not until late in the investigation of Huna that the writer discovered how badly the words used by the kahunas had been mistranslated and misunderstood. It was only then that fresh translations from the roots of the words, and studies of the symbol meanings of terms, gave an insight into the significance of observed practices. In no long time the system was uncovered in outline. Later, the information held by W. R. Stewart added greatly to the outline, especially in its theory and in the matter of the origins of Huna. Until a little headway had been made in the West toward developing the psycho-sciences, it would have been all but impossible to reconstruct Huna. However, with a partial understanding of the subconscious and conscious as parts of mind, of vital forces of two voltages, and of mesmeric and hypnotic forces of suggestion, it was possible to see that in the beliefs and practices of the kahunas (and words used by them) there were to be found definite parallels for our psychological ideas. At first an attempt was made to fit the kahuna ideas into the modern ones, but soon it was realized that the task must be reversed and modern ideas changed and expanded to fit those of the kahunas. The same thing occurred in examining the materials of Psychic Science and those Huna ideas retained in recognizable form in religions. In the New Testament there were many passages which, when Huna was understood, could be made to fit neatly into the Huna meaning. But before Huna is understood, the meaning was not such that it could be used to add clear and definitive parts to the old lore. For instance: in Luke 8:5 to 16, we read the parable of the sower and that the disciples were told, "Unto you it is given to know the mysteries of the kingdom of God: but to others in parables; that seeing they might not understand." A study of these several passages would seem to promise a glimpse of the mysteries. With knowledge of Huna one can open up the possible meaning of the parable. In the parable the sower scattered seeds, some of which fell in good soil and grew, some of which fell on barren rock and withered, and some of which fell among thorns and were crowded out. In kahuna lore we have the idea of the thought forms of prayer. These have to be carefully constructed to include no thought of doubt or fear or of a contaminating negative nature. This prayer must be planted in the correct place, or shadowy body of the High Self. If it is scattered elsewhere it falls on barren rock. If the prayer includes doubts and fears, these can be said to "crowd out" the desirable thought forms. In Hawaiian, the word for "seed" (a symbol of the thought forms) is anoano. This word and its root, ano, give several meanings when translated. The following list of meanings taken from the Hawaiian dictionary will show how this word can be used as a symbol to cover much of the mechanism of creating and offering a thought form prayer:

1. "A solemn stillness. A sacred place." (Note that this sacred place is the High Self to which the prayer is directed.)

2. "Expression of certainty of something doing or to be done." (Note the faith indicated here.)

3. "Now, at this present time, immediately." (Note the idea of the instant reaction of the High Self in answering the correctly made

prayer.)

4. "Seed or seeds." (Note: This is the basic symbol of thought forms in a prayer.)

5. (Root ano alone.) "The meaning of a word or phrase. Likeness or image of a thing. The moral quality of an action, as good or evil, or the moral state of the heart. To change or transform. To change the external appearance. To set apart or consecrate for a special purpose. Doubt or fear." (Note how these several meanings can indicate some phase of the making of the prayer thought forms. The guilt complexes are implicated in the "moral" element. The image of the thing or circumstance desired is found in the thought form prayer, which is transformed or changed into the answer to prayer, by the High Self. In making a prayer the element of fear or doubt must always be present and can never be safely ignored, for if there is a thought form of doubt or fear mingled with the prayer inadvertently, it is a sowing on barren rocks or among thistles.) Similar studies of many Hawaiian words used by the kahunas have been a great help in understanding how they thought and what they believed. Our experimental groups will have to blaze a pioneer trail through the wilderness ahead. Fortunately, the mechanisms of Huna are simple enough to be understood, and the materials upon which they rest are sufficiently logical in nature as not to cause their rejection before they are examined and compared. There is no necessity to affront our reasoning selves by a denial of the reality of the word about us. To understand the ability to see into the future we do not need to try to see time and space as a single fourth-dimensional entity. Free will and predestination need no longer be stumbling blocks. The dogmas of "sin" boil down to simple concepts, and take on new meanings since we know the nature of the complex. An experimenter may be of any religion or hold any set of scientific convictions, but will, of necessity have to set his or her previously gathered convictions to one side while considering Huna and experimenting with it. This ability to be of an open mind is important. As few of us have a natural ability to

use or produce the simple movements of thought forms, shadowy body materials, or vital forces, these abilities must be learned. There is, of course, nothing to prevent an immediate effort to contact the High Self and obtain fire-immunity or instant healing, but it is thought that, for the average person, this effort should at least be made parallel to growth in simpler abilities. Fortunately for us, these first steps are not new or incredible. There is a fine literature to tell us the experiences of others in learning to use telepathy and mind reading. We need only study those accounts and read into them the elements from Huna which better explain their mechanisms. Any library will have at least a few books on these subjects. Upton Sinclair's book, "Mental Radio", Eileen Garrett's "Telepathy" and Dunninger's "What's On Your Mind" are excellent, as are several others. Dr. Rhine's books on Extra Sensory Perception are heavier but useful. Experiments along these lines — a daily practice is indicated — will also bring some clairvoyance, in which distant scenes may be observed or visions of the future may well up from storage in the low self (or come directly from the High Self through the low self). Psychic abilities of other kinds may also begin to show themselves, and even the presence of those on the "other side" may be noticed. For those who wish to invite dreams of the future, and through them an early but unpredictable, contact with the High Self, J. W. Dunne's book, **"An Experiment with Time"**, will give a simple method which has repeatedly been demonstrated by readers on first trial. Everything is grist for the experimenter's mill. He may invent new practices to develop his abilities. There are few limitations in this new field where each individual is a pioneer. A slightly different development is needed to be able to cause the low self to protrude a part of its shadowy body to a slight, or greater, distance. The kahunas speak of this as "sticking out a finger" of the shadowy body. With this "finger" must be projected a fractional part of the five senses, which are naturally resident in the shadowy body (and which are removed from the physical body at death). These senses are usually tightly integrated with the organs of sense in the physical body, and it is only after some practice that most of us can protrude a "finger" containing some shadowy body sensory organs. This training can be begun by trying patiently to get the low self to go out and get an impression of some object concealed in a paper box or container, then bring the impression back to show the middle self. The order is, "Go sense it, and then come back and show me what it is." (One experimenter found that his low self went out to see what was in his row of small cardboard boxes, but did not understand that it had to make an image of things seen, to show to the middle self.) The low self is much like a dog who chases a ball, but does not bring it to his master until patiently coaxed. The low self is like an animal and must be treated with kindness and coaxed. If suggestion or auto suggestion is used in this training, it must be acceptable to the low self or it will reject it and refuse to take part in the work. If the work is made into a game, it will go much better. Under hypnotic influence or when in a trance condition, individuals have often been able to see with the eyes closed, or through the skin. The shadowy body of the low self can be projected to a distance during sleep to use the five senses in observing distant things. (See "Astral Projection" by Carrington and Muldoon.) The blind now are taught successfully to project "fingers" of the shadowy body to sense the location and nature of obstacles placed before them. (This adds to the theory that an echo of sound is caught by a mysteriously quickened sense of hearing and used to locate and identify the obstacles. Sound only helps in projecting the "finger" in the right way. The failure to sense obstacles in a snow storm, with a silent fall of snowflakes, may not be the fault of the silence. It may be the difficulty caused by the multiplication of small moving objects between the blind person and larger obstacles.) A "finger" can best be projected following the guidance of a shadowy thread or sound track, but can also be projected at random without them. In this projection practice, the experimental groups just formed at the time of this writing, used sets of five small pill boxes, placing a variety of small objects in them, and mixing the boxes around with closed eyes. Fingers were laid on the boxes or they were looked at from a short distance. Several experimenters learned almost at once to project a "finger" and get a sensory impression of the contents of these boxes. No one was perfect, but one young lady successfully picked out a box containing keys five times in succession. Another correctly identified five out of six objects in one try. Objects were twice correctly identified on first try from across a room. It is most exciting to find that one has these abilities and to watch them begin to develop and show themselves. (It will be still more exciting when one can place a hand over a flame and not be burned, or cause instant healing.) As experimental groups progress in their training, there will come the fascinating effort to see if we can contact the High Self and get apports, materializations — the physical phenomena of the seance room, but WITHOUT the mediation of spirits working through mediums. Experiments will be made with the curious properties of the vital force, especially as it is projected in "fingers" partly filled with ectoplasmic substance (slightly densified or thickened shadowy body material.) Baron Eugene Person demonstrated some of the curious properties of this vital force of ours. His books may be found in some libraries. Other studies of the force may be found recorded in Nandor Fodor's excellent "Encyclopedia of Psychic Science", or in some of the many books on psychic phenomena. The kahunas made use of this vital force in several ways, and we may be able to do much with it. The vital force is increased in the body by a simple act of will. A variation of the Person method works well. In it one stands with hands outstretched at the side at shoulder level, and with feet well apart. One then makes the affirmation, "I am accumulating a large extra charge of bodily vital force. I feel it tingle in my hands." One soon learns the trick, or rather one's low self learns it, and the presence of the extra charge creates a tingle in the extremities. If a person or animal is stood before one so charged, and facing away from him, hands may be placed on the person's shoulders or on the animal's rump, and, when drawn away slowly will exert a strong magnetic pull on the person or animal. There is much in this corner of the field yet to explore. Normal health and mental balance are necessary qualifications for anyone who proposes to carry on experiments. If the work leads into psychic experiences where the spirits of the dead (or low self spirits) are seen or felt, great caution should be observed and the help of an experienced medium obtained if further work in this direction is to be carried out. While lack of fear is in itself a protective element, one should know when to let well enough alone. Obsession is possible. Deep breathing exercises often help to get one ready to begin experiments. Accounts of the uses of this simple mechanism will be found in many of the books on telepathy and mind reading. Deep breathing with a willed effort to accumulate an extra charge of low vital force is good if one is to use any form of auto suggestion to try to get the low self to act as desired. The breathing is an excellent stimulus to accompany auto suggestion, as are spoken words of command. The yogis of India have learned to breathe deeply for a time and suggest themselves into a deep trance condition. It is probable that an excess charge of vital force may be taken by the middle entity and raised in voltage to use as a power in giving suggestion to the low self. The low and middle selves are driven apart by the impact of a very large charge of vital force from without. This may come from a mesmerist and need not be accompanied by the transfer of thought forms in suggestion. Hypnosis, on the other hand, uses far less vital force and either worded or silently projected thought forms of suggestions. The kahunas in Hawaii in the old days used their wills to cause very large charges of vital force (low voltage) to enter wooden sticks. They could toss these sticks at the enemy during battle and, upon contact, rendered the one touched unconscious. The American Indians had medicine men who could accumulate such a charge of vital force that, at contact through a finger placed on the chest of a strong brave, the brave would be rendered unconscious. In raising the dead, a large supply of vital force is poured from the hands into the dead body and the High Self is asked to restore the conditions necessary to life. The low and middle selves belonging to the body are called and commanded to make their way back into the body. Dr. Brigham watched this process and made note of the odd fact that the spirits (lower selves) were ordered to re-enter the body through one of the great toes. Incredible as such operations may seem to us, we must take care not to crystallize our ideas of Huna. We do not know where the limit of actions may lie, nor what limitations are natural to the High Self. By no means should we put an arbitrary limit on phenomena until there is evidential reason for doing so. The reconstructed system of Huna is a religion, as it always was in its original form. Religion is a belief in Higher Beings and a Supreme Being, as we accept the idea of religion today. But in essence religion is the science of man and his relation to Higher Beings. Huna includes all that relates to the knowledge of man and his three selves, and all that the middle self can grasp of the nature of God, even all that the High Self can reveal concerning Beings higher than itself. We will try to reconstruct Huna in its works, philosophy and organization. We will have everything but the old cult of secrecy, surely humanity has advanced to the point where all are entitled to know as much of any truth as they are able to grasp. How long it will take to complete the experimental work is hard to predict. At this writing it is just being organized. Word will have to be spread of the project and its materials. Many shoulders must be put to the wheel. Membership in the Huna Research Associates will be open to all applicants of sound mind and morals, regardless of religious or racial affiliations. Experimental members will give what time and talent they have to experimentation. Sustaining members will offer their various contributions and help, and encourage the experimenters. Associate members will do what they can, watch progress sympathetically, and spread the news of the rediscovery of the Huna system. All members will be eligible for such benefits as may be made available when and if healers are developed. In due time it is anticipated that a foundation will be established for, or within, the organization, and places be provided for all Huna related activities — teaching, publishing, and practicing the Huna system. As there is no necessity for the denial of the reality of physical or social ills, in so far as Huna is concerned, these things can be approached in the ordinary way. It is only when ordinary remedial means fail that recourse must be taken to the psycho-religious healing practices of Huna. Of course, the day may come when people learn to contact the High Self for themselves, and will heal all their ills through its help, but that day is hard to imagine. In practice, physicians of the several schools, psychologists, and healers will work together. Much of the healing done by the kahunas was of the slow or psychological kind. This form of healing may turn out to be a great help to medical, surgical and manipulative healing. Patients applying for healing will probably present medical records, and then be conditioned by psychologists to get them free from guilt and other hindering complexes. This will save the time of those who will then contact the High Self and construct the prayer for instant (or less than instant) healing. There must be no retrogression. All available knowledge must be used wherever possible. One definite innovation, however, will come in the healing of social tangles and circumstantial ills. Healing in this classification will begin directly with the use of psychological conditioning after a preliminary study of the individual case. A decision will be reached by the joint efforts of patient and psychologist as to just what changes in conditions are to be requested. After that the healer will take over to complete the work of presenting the prayer for a changed "future" to the High Self. Work under this classification is of far more importance than would appear at first glance. It has many ramifications. Its implications are great and vital to health and happiness. The prospect before us seems very bright indeed. At last we have before us a basic psycho-religious system which seems to be a serviceable restoration of Huna. We can be certain that this system was not merely a jumble of dogmas and superstitions. In it, we have at last a system known to have worked right up to modern times in the hands of the kahuna fire-walkers and healers. Even more encouraging is the fact that we have the scientific knowledge which may help us begin bringing the ancient basic system to further perfection and workability. We inherited Mathematics and Astronomy from the elder races, and we have been able to bring both to much higher stages of development. In any event, a start is being made. It may be that too few will take an interest in the project to forward it to completion. It is possible that it will have to be dropped now, and left to some future generation to take up and carry forward. On the other hand, if there are a sufficient number who can see the shining possibilities and who will set to work with a will, spreading information about Huna and the experimental project, there could result, in a very short time, an organization of such size and scope that undertakings which are impossible at the moment will quickly become accomplishments. It is greatly to be hoped that wide interest and eager enthusiasm will enable the work to move swiftly forward on such a scale that, in some one of many experimental groups, the way back to the workable Huna will quickly be demonstrated. There are so many who need help. Some cannot wait too long for it to come. Love and compassion urge us to make haste.

EPILOGUE
by Dr. E. OTHA WINGO

WHAT IS HUNA?

HUNA is a practical system of psychology long used by the kahuna of ancient Hawaii, who for centuries kept it as their carefully guarded secret. Huna, the Hawaiian word for "secret" was the name given by Max Freedom Long to the psycho-religious methods of the kahuna, or "keepers of the secret", in performing their particular kinds of "miracles" or "magic". Some of these miracles were healing the sick, solving personal problems, untangling financial and social difficulties, and changing the future for the better. It was Max Freedom Long who ferreted out these once secret methods and made them widely known throughout the world through his books and bulletins. Since at least 1936, when his first book, **RECOVERING THE ANCIENT MAGIC**, was published in England, the theories and methods of the ancient kahuna have been researched and experimented with by their discoverer and later by hundreds of Huna Research Associates throughout the world, who worked with him in testing out the principles. Today, there are **NO SECRETS**. The principles of HUNA are open to all who are willing to investigate and use them. The basic test of **HUNA** or any other system of psychology, psychic science, philosophy, or religion is whether it works. Try it. If it works, use it. If not, you can freely seek other ways of fulfilling your potential or solving your problems. But be sure that you have tried ALL the Huna ideas and concepts before rejecting them. HUNA is not an "occult" system — that is, hidden from all but a few "favored" adherents. It is based on knowledge of human psychology and of how the various parts of man function. When you learn how the psyche works, you will be able to see that it functions properly and with greatest effectiveness. HUNA emphasizes normal living in every way, and makes everyday life more livable. In times of stress, HUNA offers effective relief in any situation. As Max Freedom Long aptly put it, "If you are not using HUNA, you are working too hard!" The basic tenets of HUNA can be summarized in these words:

NO HURT: NO SIN - SERVE TO DESERVE.
Potentially, HUNA principles will work for everyone. When the desired results are not obtained, HUNA psychology reveals the causes of the failure.

IS "PSYCHIC ABILITY" NECESSARY?
No, it is not necessary to have "psychic" ability in order to use HUNA. Such ability is natural to everyone and is developed to a greater extent by some, while in others such qualities are latent, or unrecognized although used naturally. Because the principles of HUNA involve the study of universal laws and basic concepts, most people discover that the intuition becomes stronger and a sort of "psychic" or "spiritual" awareness begins to develop. This awareness is the by-product of profound study in any area — whether astrology or physics, art or the Tarot, biochemistry, psychology or HUNA.

YOU ARE MORE THAN A BODY
Because you are conscious of your own existence, you realize that you are alive and that a process of thinking is taking place. You are aware of your body and its various functions, both voluntary and involuntary. The part of you that is aware of these things — the real you, so to speak — enables you to be conscious of the fact that you exist as a spiritual or psychic "person" in addition to the body in which you seem to live. It is natural, therefore, to speak of YOU and YOUR BODY, as two parts, whether they are actually separate or not.

CONSCIOUS AND SUBCONSCIOUS MINDS
At times, a person speaks of "having a little talk with himself, "in order

to make up his mind about a decision or to work up courage for something very difficult or frightening." "I told myself there was nothing to worry about," we might say. Or, in trying to make a decision, we have a little conversation "with ourselves" and mentally list the pros and cons of the alternatives. It is as if one part of us argues for one side, while a second part comes up with the arguments for the other. Whether we consider that there are really two of us inside our minds, or two functions of one mind, at least it seems for the moment that two separate minds exist. At the time, the function of the mind is dual and not single. Since psychology recognizes a subconscious part of the mind, whether a separate mind or specialized function of a single mind, it is natural therefore to state that there are two minds or psychic entities. For the purpose of discussing the psyche, we may speak of two minds or two selves — the conscious-mind self and the subconscious-mind self. It is the conscious mind which the kahuna called uhane, or the middle self, the part of man that is conscious of his own existence and has the ability to reason. The subconscious mind was unihipili, or the low or inner self. This is the one we "have a talk with". The term "low" has no reference to rank or importance, but only to the fact that it is "below" the level of consciousness (therefore the term sub-conscious) and has its bodily center in the solar plexus (below the head). The terms "inner self", "little self", "secret self", "real self" also help to express what is meant. Remember, though, that the function of this part of you is very important and the low self has a very large part to play in your life.

THERE IS YET A THIRD PART OF MAN
The third part is the High Self — called by the kahuna by the name Aumakua. This is sometimes called the "superconscious", but writers unfamiliar with Huna may use that word to designate the subconscious. The High Self is the "older, utterly trustworthy, parental spirit". The High Self may, in religious terms, be called "God", or a sort of guardian angel, who helps us when requested to do so, but does not interfere if not

asked to help. However, the concept of "God'-' or deity was considered to be above the level of the High Self, which is an integral part of us — the spiritual part. It is the High Self that brings all desired conditions into reality. All three selves have their proper part to play in the life of each of us, and they must work together to accomplish whatever is desired, whether solving a problem in the present, or trying to work for a better future. When the three work harmoniously together, things can happen that may appear to be "miracles". But when you know the proper functions of the three selves and how they can work together, the miracles will be seen to be in no way "supernatural". If you would know what kind of person the High Self is, examine what are known as the divine qualities, in order to get some idea. The High Self expresses all of them - compassion, patience, love, forgiveness. It is a step advanced in the mental powers and creative abilities. But the ideal to which we aspire is to become a complete person, with all parts united.

THE INVISIBLE PATTERN: AKA OR SHADOWY BODIES

Now imagine that there is an original blueprint or pattern, printed on transparent material, which fits each of the three selves in every detail. Compare this with the transparent overlays used in encyclopedias to illustrate the various skeletal, muscular or nervous systems of the physical body. The kahuna of ancient Hawaii described the three selves of man with their exact duplicates or blueprints, which they referred to as **Aka-bodies.** This invisible **Aka-substance** formed a sort of invisible pattern or "aura" around each of the three selves, keeping the blueprint intact, but capable of changing shapes temporarily to form a connecting thread between the low self, middle self, and High Self. Since aka has a sticky quality and stretches without breaking, when contact is made between two people, a long, sticky thread is drawn out between the two, like a thin spider-web, and the connection between them remains. Further contacts add other aka-threads and these are braided together into an a/ca-cord, resulting in strong rapport between the two persons.

Such an aka-cord must be kept strongly braided between the low self and the middle self, and between the low self and the High Self, in order for the three to work together harmoniously.

THE TRIANGLE OR TRINITY
The symbol of the triangle suggests that once all three selves are working together with perfect union and harmony, we have perfect communication among the three selves.

MANA OR VITAL FORCE
The kahuna recognized the magnetic and the opposite, repelling nature of vital force, or mana, but unfortunately, they left no detailed exposition of the subject. They knew the force as a thing which had to do with all thought processes and bodily activity. It was the essence of life itself. The kahuna symbol for this life force was water. Water flows and so does the vital force. Water fills things. So does the vital force. Water may leak away — so may vital force. All thinking involves an electrical-like activity of the higher voltage of vital force. The kahuna associated all thinking processes with mana. The word mana-o means "thinking, the o added to show that the process is one of using mana to produce thought. As each thought is formed, it is given its shadowy (aka) body and is fastened by a thread of the same substance to thoughts which came before it (association of ideas in terms of modern psychology). Mana is taken from the food and air by the low self and is stored in its aka body, but it is shared with the middle self and with the High Self. The mana, when used as the life force of the middle self is changed in some subtle way. The kahuna of old symbolized this as a dividing of the basic mana into two kinds, and called it mana-mana — indicating by doubling the word the fact that is was doubled in power, so that it could be used by the middle self to command and control the low or inner self. This is the force we know vaguely in modern psychology as "the will". It is also the force which should at all times be

strong enough to make the low self carry out every suggestion. It is seldom used in its full strength, and so the low self gets out of hand or flits from one activity to another, without carrying out any suggestion or command fully.

ACCUMULATING A SURCHARGE OF MANA
It is not generally known that we can use certain exercises to accumulate a surcharge — an extra-large and powerful charge — of vital force at any time we need it, providing we are in fair health and are not starved. We can use these surcharges of mana in several very valuable ways, particularly in healing ourselves and others, and in making a prayer/action that will have real power.

AN ACTION OF THE MIND
The kahuna believed that by an action of the mind a man adds to the amount of mana he has already created from food and air consumed, by quickening the extraction process. This theory is supported by our physiologists, who have found that when we digest our food it is not all used at once, but is changed to blood sugar (glycogen) and oxidized with oxygen from the air we breathe to give us such amounts of force and energy as we may need for the work we happen to do. If this is true (and there seems no reason to question these findings) the low self, who attends to all such matters, can at any time begin to take in more air and cause more blood sugar to be burned to create more of that strange chemically-manufactured force we call MANA. The low self learns to do this in most cases with very little trouble.

THE ACCUMULATION OF A SURCHARGE OF VITAL FORCE is accomplished simply by explaining to the low self within just what it is to do, and then asking it to try to do it. To help the low self, we can use the voluntary muscles and start breathing more deeply. This will furnish the air to be used, as well as suggest what we want done.

THE MANA RISES LIKE A FOUNTAIN

The kahuna used the symbol of water for mana. When they wished to accumulate a surcharge, they breathed deeply and visualized mana rising like water rises in a fountain, higher and higher until it overflows. The body is pictured as the fountain and the water is the mana.

AN EXERCISE

Exercise or any form of physical exertion always starts the low self to manufacturing more mana or vital force; otherwise we would use up what we have in a few moments and would begin to feel faint. Every athlete knows that he can go only so far and so fast on his first wind, which is the charge of mana he happens to have in the body and aka body at the start — but that in a short time he gets a fresh supply of strength (his second wind) and can then keep going steadily and at top speed.

OR A MENTAL ATTITUDE

Instead of exercising, we can assume the mental attitude of one getting set to run a race. We hold the picture in mind of getting ready to run, we breathe more rapidly and tense up the muscles a little. The low self seldom fails to get the idea then, and will begin creating the desired vital force.

A SENSE OF WELL-BEING

The person with a low normal charge-level of vital force has almost always found that he can sense the additional surge of mana after taking on an extra supply. It adds to the sense of well-being, of physical strength, or will and determination, and it sharpens the mind, makes memorization faster and easier, and the senses more acute. This can easily be tested by checking the clearer vision or sharper memory after a surcharge of vital force. All evidence shows that the mana is indeed the life force and that with it the life is strong, while without it, life fades.

MANA AND "MIRACLES"
However, the point that is most important when considering mana or vital force is that when one has learned to accumulate a surcharge, it is possible to use, with the help of the High Self, to perform "miracles" which range all the way from slow and simple healing to miraculous changes in bodily tissues and even in the fabric of the future.

DURING SLEEP
The High Self contacts us of its own accord in our sleep, making use, so the kahuna thought, of the connecting aka-cord. Our thoughts of the day, with our plans, hopes, fears, loves and hates, are examined, taken (perhaps as duplicated thought forms), and at the time vital force is taken. This vital force is stepped up to the high "voltage" (in the analogy of electricity) and is used by the High Self to construct a shadowy (aka) body which will materialize as part of our future. Such thought forms were described by the kahuna as "seeds" and were symbolized by seeds which were vitalized by the High Self and grew into actualities of the future.

"LET THE RAIN OF BLESSINGS FALL!"
The High Self not only takes from us the vital force or mana that it needs, but returns a compensating force to us. This is vital to our health and well-being. This return is pictured as a shower of mana falling from the up-welling fountain, as a "rain of "blessings". After contact with the High Self for the purpose of sending a gift of mana, and also presenting a "prayer picture", the kahuna ended his prayer with these words: "The prayer takes its flight. Let the rain of blessings fall." Daily contact and guidance in all of our lives may be had from the High Self — but only if asked for. All the more reason to discover for yourself the basic

concepts of Huna psychology and how they may be put to practical use in your own life — the three selves and their functions as a unified team and the importance of understanding how mana, the life force, can be increased and utilized to bring about for you a better life now and for the future.

Made in the USA
Columbia, SC
11 March 2021

34332231R00039